I Sleep in the Stars

Written and Illustrated by Phil Hammett

Author's Note:

Hopefully, I've found the right balance between imagination and science

because I believe in both equally.   Science? Yes, actually Cepheus' words

were inspired by a great chemist. (See notes in the back.)

I wanted to focus on the importance of finding one's "inner star"

or higher self, which resides in the subconscious mind.   Building this internal relationship is

a life-long journey but well worth the trip.   I believe it's an essential part of our lives.

People might wonder if this is beyond the capabilities of young children, but I say childhood

is the perfect time to start.   Indeed, sometimes as children we seem to have more insight than

adults, but rational thinking about the physical world can cause intuition to wither from lack of use.

We must exercise both modes of thought- rational and intuitive.

Above all, enjoy!   And... check the back of the book for notes on:

Imagination- finding images hidden in the clouds

Wonder- finding constellations in the night scenes

When most people sleep,

they say their heads are in the clouds.

But not me.   I *live* in the clouds,

so when I sleep... I sleep in the stars.

"How can you live in the clouds?"

you might ask. "Wouldn't you fall through?"

Well, the secret to living in the clouds

is in our cloud castles.

Cloud castles are made of a special

material known only to cloud people.

It is so light, that it floats on clouds

like oil on water.

Yet it is strong, strong enough to walk on.

Clouds seem like puff-balls in the sky,

but they contain tons of water.

Next time it rains, think of how

heavy that rainwater must be.

And so those clouds can easily

support the weight of our cloud castles.

I am Andri, and I live in a cloud castle.

I love to sleep because I love to dream.

In my dreams I can fly.

I often fly across vast parts of the Earth.

"At night while I lie dreaming,

the sky surrounds my head,

I stretch my mind beyond all time,

this body I do shed.

I cannot gauge the distance; I never know how far.

My home is the Universe.

I sleep in the stars."

I stretch my mind beyond all time,

This body I do shed.

And when I wake up, I *still* want to fly,
so I settle for the next best thing- dancing!
When I hear the morning music drifting
through my window from the plaza below,
I run down the steps.
The band in the plaza plays songs
that both wake up cloud people
and make them want to dance.

This morning as I dance, one song
seems to be shorter than usual.
As the band ends the song,
I hear murmuring. Then they
begin playing a very special tune-
the call for a dragon-riders' meeting!
Cepheus (*See*-fee-us), the dragon-rider teacher,
is calling the meeting, and that includes me. I'm in!

Dragon-riders have a very special job.
They guide dragons to keep our cloud castles
in the right place.   And the job of guiding dragons
has to be done by younger cloud people, because
they are best at making friends with dragons.

For years I had watched dragons
and their riders fly over the castle grounds,
and I wished that I could be up there
gliding through the air, just like in my dreams.
After years of learning to ride and learning to
direct dragons, I became a dragon-rider.

My dragon, Uccello (Oo-_chey_-low), is very powerful
and smart for a dragon. When I'm riding Uccello,
I feel like he is a part of me and I am a part of him.

I sit in a pocket on the back of Uccello's neck and strap myself in.
Cepheus told us that we can never, never take off the strap while in the air!

One time when Uccello and I were near the equator, we came upon the Doldrums. The Doldrums is a stream of air around the center of the Earth where the heat makes the air rise straight up. The wind turns from going across the water, to going upward. This was a problem for ancient sailors; they couldn't sail their ships upward!   But for birds, this rising air is like a vacation; it gives them a lift without having to flap their wings.

When Uccello and I approached the Doldrums, we saw a vast number of seagulls playing in the rising air. They rode the air up, and then glided around in spirals, circling back so they could float up again in the rising air, like riding a rollercoaster.

When Uccello saw this, he wasted no time diving into the rising air.   I felt a surge of wind blowing us upward!   We floated up and circled around, just like the seagulls. For hours we glided in the rising air. It was a blast!

But now I'm anxious to find out about the meeting, so I run to the tower 10

where the dragon-riders meet. Other riders seem to be in a rush as well. When we settle in, the room is alive with conversations about our drought. "My Dad says that our crops are wilting," says one. "I haven't had a bath in weeks," says another. "You never take baths!" responds his friend. Bursts of laughter follow. I smile, but I start to think about what we might have to do to solve the water problem.

When Cepheus arrives, the room becomes quiet.   He starts with an old quote, "Water, water, everywhere, but not a drop to drink."*

I realize that he is using the line from the poem of a sailor who couldn't drink any of the seawater around him.   Cepheus knows that's like our problem as cloud people. We are surrounded by the water in clouds, but we can't drink them! There is only one source of water for us, rain.

"This is a serious thing for us," Cepheus continues, "and we need the help of dragon-riders to solve the problem.   I know where there is a rainstorm," he adds, "but the rain is too far away for us to drag the castles; it's beyond the curvature of the Earth."

*The Rime of the Ancient Mariner

"We must use the vessica,
and we must hurry!" he adds.
I can sense the riders
getting nervous, as they
whisper to each other.

We have all been trained to use
the vessica, a large stretchy tarp
that is carried by four dragons
and their riders. It is very rare
that this is necessary.
Only the most experienced
riders would go on this mission.
We anxiously await who he will choose.

Cepheus explains that four of us must leave just before nightfall in order to reach the storm in time. One of us must be an expert navigator.

He has always said that I had a natural talent for navigation, but there are others who are older and have been training much longer than I have. Among the group of dragon-riders is Perseo, who started training before I did.   Perseo has been friendly and helpful to me, but I think he feels that boys are better dragon-riders than girls.   A very skilled rider, he is most certain to be one of those chosen.

Two riders whom I'm not familiar with are chosen first, then Perseo. "And the fourth rider will be Andri!" Cepheus exclaims.   I can scarcely contain my excitement! My heart starts beating more quickly; I feel honored to be chosen to go on such an important mission. The others look at me in amazement, and I try not to notice.   But their surprise leaps even higher when Cepheus adds, "And Andri will also be the chief navigator."   I hear a faint, "What?" in the background.

A grin stretches across my face, but I feel a little embarrassed at all the looks I am getting from the group of riders.   I try not to let that show because I need to prove to them that I am up to the task of chief navigator. I feel like I need to be serious.

Cepheus gives instructions to the other dragon-riders on helping prepare for our trip, and then he asks me and Perseo to stay for our special instructions.   He gives me the sextant and compass I will need to navigate the stars. Perseo gets the telescope that he will need. Now we must try to get some sleep because much of the journey will be at night. After Perseo leaves, I ask Cepheus why he chose me to be chief navigator. "There is more to navigating than reading instruments," he says. "You must be in touch with your inner star, and you my dear, are the best at that."   The warmth in his voice soothes me. "Now you must get some sleep before the journey," he adds.

You might wonder how Cepheus knows where the rainstorm is.   Well, he is not only a dragon-rider trainer but also a scientist.   He has a fabulous laboratory with a telescope and a giant compass. Brass rings surround the glass that protects the surface. The pointer is a huge magnet of shiny steel with a bluish tint. In the middle of the pointer is the shape of a bird, cast in gold, whose wings stretch toward the ends of the pointer.

I once asked Cepheus what kind of bird it was, and he told me it was a seagull.   When I asked him why, he said, "Never better is the day, when we go to where the seagulls play." I thought of Uccello and me riding the air with the gulls, and I smiled.

Cepheus' telescope will only view what is before the horizon, before the curvature of the Earth blocks our view. But perhaps the most unusual thing about Cepheus is his ability to "see" beyond the curvature of the Earth.   Cepheus can put himself into a state of mind where he can see things other cloud people can't.   He says anyone can do it, but I've tried, and it doesn't seem possible to me.   Remember when I said I sleep in the stars?   Well, Cepheus can put his head in the stars whenever he needs to.   He often says,

"To all my friends and those of youth,

We must find dreams that hold the truth."

S
SW
W
NW

As I lie down to rest for the journey, I think of what Cepheus had said about my inner star. I recall a dream that I had told him about: In this dream I was flying, but not over the Earth; I was traveling through the stars!   One star seemed quite close, but as I approached it, I realized it wasn't a star like the sun, that would be way too hot to get close to.   I felt that this was my star.   I was a little bit scared at first, but its gentle beauty soon calmed me.

This star was a glowing light, but it began changing right before my eyes. It became a beautiful flower.   A bee was approaching the flower bringing it pollen.   Then the star changed back to its original glow.   I woke up feeling mystified.

Cepheus explained to me that this was a message from my "inner star."   He said I should figure out the message on my own.   Then he added, "What do bees do for plants?"

I thought about how bees carry pollen from one flower to the next so that the plant can grow fruit or seeds.   Maybe my star was telling me it would help me grow just like bees help the plants grow.   When I told Cepheus this, he smiled.

"You are growing quite nicely," he said quietly.

I think about my inner star dream and it helps me relax.   Cepheus told us to repeat
something meaningful over and over in our minds.   I choose his
saying about dreams that hold the truth, and I keep saying it in my mind, "For all my
friends and those of youth, we must find dreams that hold the truth."
I gradually slip off to sleep.

Suddenly, Uccello and I are flying through the sky.
We appear to be on the upcoming journey
racing through the clouds.   I notice that
one of the clouds has a strange shape to it,
almost human, but it is holding a curved object
in an outstretched arm.   Now I see that
it is an archer.   As I watch more closely,
the archer pulls back his bow and aims an arrow
straight at Uccello and me!   I wake and sit straight up.

I look out the window.   The sun is getting low in the sky, and I know it is time to get

ready to go.   I race down to tell Cepheus about my new dream. He nods, and softly states,

"That was a message from your inner star."   Then in a concerned voice, he adds,

"I think you know what this means, don't you?"   I pause for a few seconds,

"Zilches!" I blurt out.   All this time I had been trying to deny it.

"And you remember the trick I taught you?"

"Yes, but the others must follow..."

"They will follow," he says with certainty,

"And remember, remain open to your inner star."

Zilches are weird, massive water creatures who seem
to spend their time making people's lives miserable.
Their watery stretched-out bodies are dark and spooky
in appearance, but their heads are very small and are
hidden by water vapor. They're called Zilches because
with their tiny heads, they don't have much for brains, zilch.

The extra dragon riders have prepared provisions for the long trip.   The dragons   20
and vessica are ready to go.   "When you get to the storm, there may be danger,"
Cepheus declares to all of us. "You all must follow Andri and Uccello carefully."
Then he turns to me as if I should speak.   At first my voice starts to break,
but I take a deep breath, clear my throat, and put a renewed energy into my voice.
"My star has shown me that there will be Zilches!" I shout firmly, "We will enter the
clouds from above and spiral in the same direction as the storm." I motion with my arm.
"Let's practice!"

We mount our magnificent creatures, and with little fanfare, I thrust my arm upward, call to
Uccello, and the dragons begin running toward the edge of the main plaza. When we reach
the edge, their wings are outstretched, and I feel the rush of wind as we are airborne! I have
Uccello climb as fast as I know the dragons are able, and the others follow us. When we are
high enough above the castle, I give the same spiral motion with my arm as I had earlier.
With the dragons instructed to glide, we form a giant spiral downward, just like we will
have to do when we reach the storm.   It is a little shaky at first, but by the second round,
we are in perfect formation.

"Wooo hooo!" shouts Perseo. I look back to see the others smiling. Cepheus's words come back to me, "They will follow."   When our gliding spiral reaches the level of the castle, I look over to see Cepheus raising his staff in triumphant approval.

With renewed hope and excitement, we head toward the horizon. According to Cepheus's instruction, we are headed in the exact direction of the raincloud.   I line up the mark on the compass with the direction of Uccello's head.   I look over at Perseo as we drift through the air, and he is all smiles, pointing the telescope at the horizon, then over at me. I laugh, glad that he's enjoying himself.   But soon it will be dark, and we will be flying by moonlight.

The yellow moon allows us to see as if it were twilight. The stars also help to light our way. Marveling at the points of shining light above, I try to make out the constellations that I know. This helps pass the time.   I keep checking the sextant and my glowing compass. We are getting close to the equator, mid-point on this amazing globe. When we are high enough, I instruct Uccello to glide, so the dragons can save their energy. Now when I look at Perseo, he seems more serious.   I think of my dream and the possibility of Zilches, and I wonder if he is feeling some of the fear that I feel.

The night seems as endless as the starry sky is wide, but I know we are traveling toward the sunrise at an amazing speed.   Eventually, we start to see signs of the glow of daylight.

I remember that it is really the Earth turning that makes it look like the sun is rising.   I think of how we are turning quietly toward the sun, even faster than we are flying.   I feel thankful to be a part of this amazing planet.

I look over at Perseo, and he is studying the horizon with the telescope.   Suddenly, he lets out a dog-like yelp!   I look in the direction where he is pointing.   Very faintly, I see a grey puff of clouds that breaks the clean line of the horizon.   We have found the rainclouds!   I adjust our course and we head swiftly in that direction.

The morning light makes it easier to see the clouds as we approach.   I know we shouldn't go too deep into the storm, for there will be more danger there.   Still, we must go deep enough to fill the vessica with water.

Now I can see the stringy grey strands hanging from the bottom of the clouds, the Zilches! Also, the flashes of light!   Their flaming arrows are part fire and part electrical shock. If you get hit by one, it burns and shocks you, and it must be taken out immediately.

We are slightly above the rainclouds now, and I can see multiple signs of Zilches.   26
The clouds are teaming with bursts of flaming arrows, and the claps of thunder make
me cringe with each strike. I try to choose a spot that has less lightning but plenty of rain.
I know the longer we wait, the more likely we are to be discovered.   I raise my arm and
give the motion, yelling to Uccello to spiral. We pierce the wispy edge of the dark clouds.

Suddenly, I can barely see through the greyish fog.   I look over towards Perseo, and all
I see is the shadowy figure of his dragon.   The two riders trailing us have vanished in
the mist, but I can see that the vessica is still stretched correctly. We are dropping quickly,
and we soon come out below the clouds, where the rain is beating down.

Now that we are below the clouds, I can see the two riders behind us buffeted by the winds.
The vessica is filling nicely, and we shall be able to make short work of this miserable task.

Zing! A burst of light flashes on Perseo's dragon, lighting up our entire group. The Zilches
have discovered us!   Luckily, the arrow bounces harmlessly off the dragon's scales, but
within a few minutes, more arrows come our way.   We have clear shields that we use
to protect us from the Zilches' arrows, and immediately we raise them into place.

Crackling, sparkling flashes of light whiz by.
Our spiral seems to be throwing off the Zilches,
but arrows are coming way too close, some bouncing
off dragon's scales, and some sizzling into the water
in the vessica. I decide that we must fly out of the storm.
Whatever water we've got will have to be enough.
I give the signal and the command to Uccello to
straighten out and fly toward safety.

Zing zing! An arrow comes straight toward me and Uccello,
just like in my dream! This one hits Uccello in the shoulder,
right between his scales! Instead of bouncing off, it sticks there!
I can feel the heat from the flames, and the vibration from the electricity.
Uccello lets out a cry of pain; this is the first time I have ever heard him make
that screeching noise. I must do something, but the arrow is too far for me to reach.

I can see that Uccello is having trouble with his left wing. The wing starts to fold
in, then it flutters up and down.

Without that wing, he will not be able to control his flight, and we could all fall into the ocean below.   But I don't think about this.   I feel the pain of that arrow as if it is in my own body.   We are one when we fly, one body and one mind, and that body is in pain and danger!

To reach the arrow, I must take off my safety strap. Sorry Cepheus!   But I can't risk losing my grip, so I slip my hand through the metal buckle even though the pin digs into my palm.   I dangle below my seat and push my knee against Uccello's scales. Avoiding the dangerous tip and the rising heat, I grasp the shank of the arrow and pull, but the arrow only wiggles.   I have to let go.

My anger about the creatures that caused this overcomes me.   "ZILCHES!" I cry out with all my breath.   I yank the arrow with a strength I didn't know I had. The arrow rips out of the scales, and I quickly drop it to avoid the flaming tip. As it hits the water below, the hot arrow screeches like an angry cat.

Perseo knows we are in trouble, so he brings his dragon closer to us. He tells his   30
dragon to hold the vessica closer to Uccello to relieve some of the weight from him.
Perseo's eyes are wide with amazement. I can tell that he feels for us like I feel for Uccello.

We have drifted a safe distance from the storm, but I can see that Uccello still does not
have full control over his wing.   We are rocking back and forth, up and down.   I tell
Uccello to glide, so we are steadier.   But I wonder how he will be able to make the long
journey home, especially with the extra weight of the water in the vessica.   We can only
glide for so long before ending up in the ocean below.

It has been many hours since we rested, and I feel exhausted.   I put my head down to
collect my thoughts.   As I close my eyes, my brain starts buzzing.   I feel like my head is
'in the stars'.   I see clouds before me, but they are rapidly changing shape. One cloud
has the shape of a seagull, and it gets clearer.   Now I can hear the voice of Cepheus,
"Never better is the day, when we go to where the seagulls play."

I sit up with a jolt. Surely this is not a time to play, but Uccello needs a rest.   We must go
to where the seagulls play!   I call to Perseo, "South to the Doldrums!" and I signal to the
others. I tell Uccello to turn left, easy because his right wing is stronger now. "Uccello, the
seagulls!" I cry. He understands.   The ride is rough, but he knows that soon he will be
able to glide and rest.

As we approach the Doldrums, I can feel the rush of air coming from below.   I tell Uccello to glide, and his wings stretch out as our flight gets smoother.   Now, instead of gliding downward, we are drifting upward!   I hear him let out a long "Aaargh" of relief.

Now that we are riding the rising air, we turn to the west.   We will continue gliding in the uplifting air until it's time to head north to our castle. Perseo is grinning with glee, and the dragons seem to be talking to each other in joyful tones.

After many hours, I can see by the sun that it is time to head north to our castle.   I can almost hear Cepheus's voice saying, "Home now."   After the gliding rest, Uccello is using his left wing almost as well as his right.   Perseo is actively searching with his telescope, and It's not long before he spots our castle in the distance.   We all give a cheer of delight, "Oooo-weee!"

Cepheus, having a much more powerful telescope, sees us way before we see the castle. As we approach, throngs of cloud people gather in the main courtyard, and their whistles and cheers fill the air. We can't pause or slow down, though, until we reach the reservoir where our dwindling water is stored. As we pass over the buildings, people are peering up out of windows.   Perseo can't resist jerking the vessica a little to splash his friends looking up from below.

As we reach the reservoir, I give the signal to Perseo, and we let go of our end of the vessica.   The tarp drops, sending tons of water crashing into the surface below.   It sounds like the ocean, only many times louder.   A tidal wave rushes up the sides and curls back toward the center. The rear riders hover to let the rest of the water drain.

Perseo and I circle around toward the courtyard and the others soon follow. As we approach, the crowd quickly scatters to make space. We touch down and Uccello lets out a roar of victory, "YEEEAARRRGH!!"   The crowd laughs and cheers at the same time. I give that giant dragon a giant hug, "You were amazing, Uccello!"

After the excitement cools down and people disperse, Cepheus asks to meet with us.
"Bravo, bravo! There will be a great celebration tonight with the queen and king!" he says.
Then he turns to me.   "Andri, that was a brave move when you pulled out the arrow,"
he said. "And you got my message. You knew to fly to the Doldrums."
"Yes. How did you know?" I inquired.   He smiled, "I can see more
in the stars than just rainclouds. But I see with my mind, not my eyes,
just like you do.   I wouldn't send you into danger without any help.
When I realized what you had done, I knew I had chosen
the right navigator for the job."
And then he added:

"To all my friends and those of youth,
You must find dreams that hold the truth."*

*See the notes in the following pages.

The Beginning-

(Here older readers can help with the words, and younger readers can help with imagining.)

Instead of "the end," this can be the beginning of perhaps using more imagination to see things in the clouds, discovering more wonder by gazing at the stars, and perhaps connecting to one's own inner star.

Every painting, every song, every building, every business, starts with imagination.   So why is it that children are so often told to focus on the "real" world?   Both concepts are important.   We need to imagine, but we need science and knowledge to bring our imaginings to fruition, so why not develop both skills?   This book could be the start of developing skills that are often forgotten. "Use them or lose them."

* But first a note about Cepheus' saying, "To all my friends and those of youth, you must find dreams that hold the truth."   This was inspired by the great chemist Fredrich Kekule.   After wracking his brain trying to figure out the chemical structure for benzene, he fell asleep and dreamt of a snake eating its tail (a message from his inner star and also an ancient symbol).   He quickly realized the circular structure of benzene, and this also opened up a new field in chemistry.   When he presented his solution to his fellow chemists, he said, "Let us learn to dream, gentlemen; then we shall perhaps find the truth."   (Quote from *Principles of Organic Chemistry*)

<u>Cover note</u>- Above the symbolic "dream star" is the constellation Andromeda (the name means "leader of humankind").   In the ancient myth, Andromeda was tragically chained to the rocks to be sacrificed to a pesky sea monster.   Luckily, Perseus saved the day by turning the monster into stone.   But in this story, Andri plays the role of rescuer.   Human consciousness has evolved since the ancient myths.   Andri has a more deserving role- intuitive, intelligent, caring, and healing.   In fact, whether man or woman, we need to embrace the female archetype (principles) of compassion and caring to make this world a better place.

Besides the constellation Andromeda, there are several more- Leo above the Sphynx, Virgo- the nurturer (p17br), Sagittarius, the benevolent archer with a warning message, not a Zilch! (p18), Aquarius, at the tip of the dragon's tail (p25).   Above the banquet, a star map begins with the Big Dipper; the ladle points to the North Star (above the pointy post); Draco snakes between the dippers. Beyond the North Star is Cepheus (transformed in this story from terrible king to wise scientist); below him is the "W" of Cassiopeia; below her, Perseus and Andromeda to the right.

I'll let you find the images within the clouds. Many happened by chance, but here are some that were intentional: Page 11- (Cepheus is making the ASL sign for "W" signifying water.) In the sky is a jug similar to that used by Aquarius in the myth of the water-bearer. On page 13, the jug appears to have water flowing out of it- the hope of success. Page 15- You'll discover many images in the lab with Cepheus.   Most notable is the seagull, (used again on page 31), and the dragon's head.   Page 25- How many other mysterious creatures can you find in the image below?

For more information and resources to help with your inner journeys please see the Facebook page "I Sleep in the Stars."